WHERE'S PETER RABBIT?

a lift-the-flap book

From *The Tale of Peter Rabbit*
The original and authorized edition
BEATRIX POTTER ™

F. WARNE & Cº

Once upon a time there were four little Rabbits, and their names were Flopsy, Mopsy, Cotton-tail and Peter. They lived with their Mother in a **sand-bank**, under the root of a tree.

'Now, my dears,' said old Mrs. Rabbit
one morning, 'you may go into the
fields or down the lane, but don't go
into Mr. McGregor's garden.'

Flopsy, Mopsy, and Cotton-tail, who
were good little bunnies, went down the
lane to gather blackberries.

Mrs. Rabbit took a **basket** and her
umbrella, and went through the wood
to the baker's.

But Peter, who was very naughty, ran straight away to Mr. McGregor's garden, and squeezed under the gate! First he ate some lettuces and some French beans; and then he ate some radishes; and then, feeling rather sick, he went round a **cucumber frame** to look for some parsley.

Mr. McGregor jumped up and ran after Peter. Peter was most dreadfully frightened and rushed all over the garden, among the **cabbages** and **potatoes**.

Unfortunately he ran right into a **gooseberry net**, and got caught by the large buttons on his jacket. Mr. McGregor came up with a sieve which he intended to pop over Peter.

Peter wriggled out just in time, leaving his jacket behind him. He rushed into the tool-shed where Mr. McGregor kept his **flower-pots** and **watering-can**.

Presently Peter
sneezed, 'Kertyschoo!'
and Mr. McGregor was after
him. Peter jumped out of a
window, but the window was too
small for Mr. McGregor. He went
back to his work.

Peter tried to find his way straight
across the garden. He came to a **pond**
where a white cat was sitting very, very still
staring into the water.

Suddenly, quite close
to him, Peter heard the
noise of a hoe – scr-r-ritch,
scratch, scratch, scritch. It was
Mr. McGregor hoeing onions.
And beyond him, at the end of the
black-currant bushes, was the gate!

Peter slipped
underneath the gate, and
was safe at last in the wood
outside the garden. He never
stopped running or looked behind him
till he got home.

That evening Peter didn't feel very
well. His mother put him to **bed**, and
gave him a dose of camomile tea.

But Flopsy, Mopsy and Cotton-tail had bread
and milk and blackberries for supper.